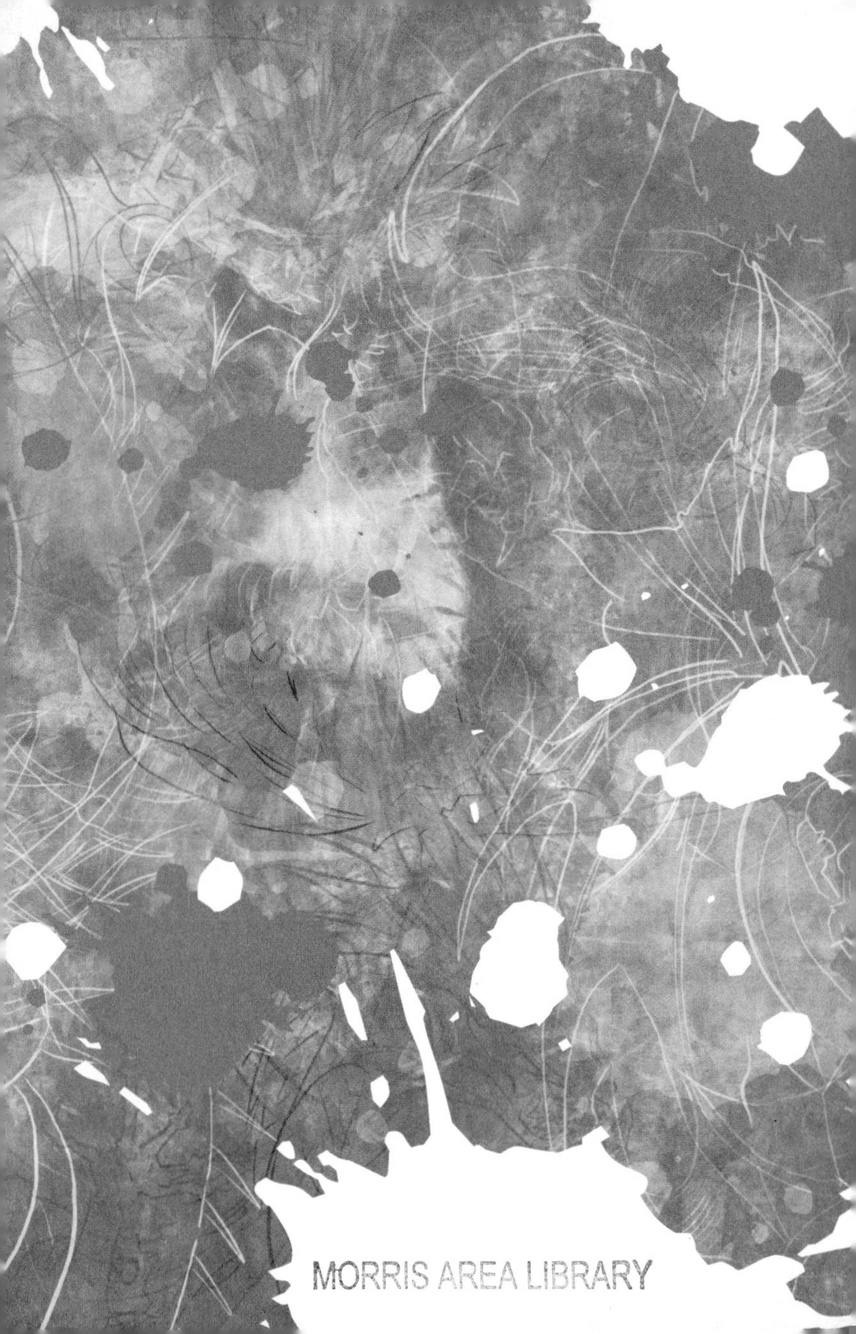

DRAGONBLOOD
Claws in the Snow

Michael Dahl

Tou Vue

STONE ARCH BOOKS
www.stonearchbooks.com

Zone Books are published by
Stone Arch Books
151 Good Counsel Drive, P.O. Box 669
Mankato, Minnesota 56002
www.stonearchbooks.com

Library of Congress Cataloging-in-Publication Data
Dahl, Michael.
    Claws in the Snow / by Michael Dahl; illustrated by
Tou Vue.
    p. cm. — (Zone Books. Dragonblood)
    ISBN 978-1-4342-1262-7 (library binding)
    [1. Dragons—Fiction. 2. Brothers—Fiction. 3. Storms—
Fiction.] I. Vue, Tou, ill. II. Title.
PZ7.D15134Cl 2009
[Fic]—dc22   2008031278

Summary: Will and his mom are caught in a blinding
blizzard. A shadow is hiding in the snow. A shadow that
roars. Giant claws grip the car. Will wishes his older and
stronger brother was with them now. Maybe he is! . . .

Creative Director: Heather Kindseth
Graphic Designer: Brann Garvey

1 2 3 4 5 6 14 13 12 11 10 09

TABLE OF CONTENTS

Introduction

A new Age of Dragons is about to begin. The powerful creatures will return to rule the world once more, but this time will be different. This time, they will have allies. Who will help them? Around the world, some young humans are making a strange discovery. They are learning that they were born with dragon blood – blood that gives them amazing powers.

CHAPTER 1
Left Behind

A teenage boy stood next to a car in a driveway.

"Your father will be sorry you couldn't come," said the boy's mother. Her hands were on the steering wheel.

"You look terrible, Henry," the little boy in the front seat told the older boy.

"I feel terrible," said Henry, rubbing his arm.

"Go back to bed," said his mother. "It's just the flu. You can call your father tomorrow and wish him a **happy birthday**."

Will, the younger boy, handed his brother a **comic book.**

"You can have this," Will said. It was a new comic. Will hadn't even read it yet.

"Thanks," said Henry. "I'll give it back when I'm done."

The older boy *walked* weakly toward the house. The car backed down the driveway and drove off.

CHAPTER 2
Snow

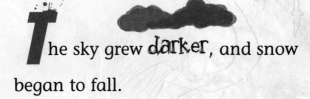

The sky grew darker, and snow began to fall.

Soon, snow blanketed the road.

More snow blew onto the windshield of the car.

"I think I should pull over," said Will's mom.

The car pulled into a small gas station.

A **dark figure** sat inside the station, staring at them.

"Wait here, Will," said his mother.

As she walked into the station, Will watched the Swirling snow.

CHAPTER 3

The White Thing

The light from the gas station formed a small, *warm circle*.

Outside the circle, the snow became thicker and wilder.

Will wiped off the window.

He kept watching the snow.

Why was his mother taking so long?

Will heard a sound. It reminded him of **thunder**.

Then he saw a shape moving through the falling snow.

A white shape with **wings** 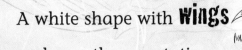 passed over the gas station.

Will jumped out of the car to get
a better look.

"**Will,**" cried his mother,
running toward him. "Back in the
car. We're going."

His mother drove out of the gas
station.

"That man was not very
helpful," she told Will.

"He said we already passed the street your father lives on," Will's mother said.

"I'm sure he's wrong," she added.

Will's father had moved to another town.

This was the first time Will and his mother were visiting the new house.

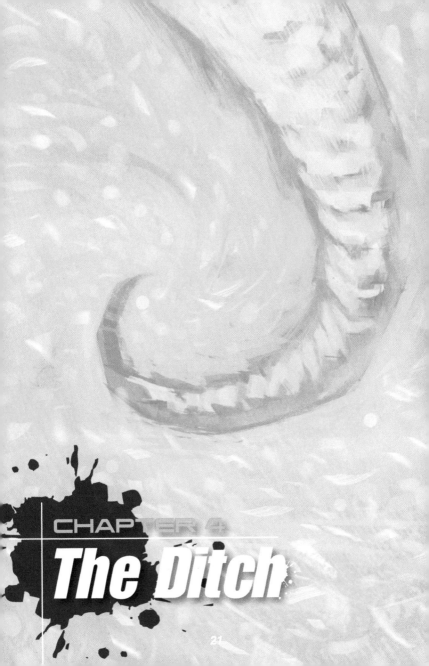

CHAPTER 4

The Ditch

"There's something out there," said Will, quietly.

"What are you talking about?" asked his mother.

The snow was so heavy they could not see the road ahead of them.

"Oh great," said his mother. "The heater's broken!"

Will felt the car begin to **swerve**.

"Hold on!" shouted his mother.

CRUNCH!

The car slid into a snowy ditch.

"Will! You're bleeding," said
his mother. He had hit his head
against the window.

His mother couldn't find her
cell phone. It had fallen out of her
purse when the car **crashed** into
the ditch.

Will's head began to **throb** with pain.

We'll be stuck here forever, he thought.

If only Henry were here, he could help us.

CHAPTER 5

Getting A Lift

The car **rocked**.

"What's going on?" said his
mother.

Will looked out. He saw a *claw*
gripping one of the car windows.

His mother **screamed**.

Will thought he heard his name.

Then something whispered,

"Will, it's me!"

The car was lifted into the air.

The car swayed back and forth in the snowy wind.

Will's mother clung tightly to him.

Then, with a bump, the car was back on the ground.

A *light* shined in front of them.

A man walked out of a lighted house. He walked toward their car.

It was Will's father.

"We're here!" shouted Will.

"Did Henry come with you?" asked Will's father.

His mother was too shocked to speak.

Will followed his parents toward the house.

A dark shape in the snow caught his eye.

It was his **comic book.**

Somewhere in the storm above them, a fierce, happy roar shook the sky.

Of Dragons and Near-Dragons

If dragons truly lived on Earth, they would belong to the reptile family. Can reptiles survive through cold winters?

Reptiles cannot produce their own body heat. They must rely on outside sources like the Sun and warm air. In the winter, many reptiles hibernate. They stay in a sleepy state for many months, until the spring returns.

Sea turtles migrate to escape the cold weather. They swim to warmer water in the southern hemisphere.

Lizards dig deep below the surface of the earth. They sleep in burrows or holes while the ground above them is frozen.

Some sand lizards hibernate below the ground until March or April. When they first come out of their holes, they look tired and pale. In a few weeks, after being in the sun, the lizards' skin turns a bright, healthy green.

ABOUT THE AUTHOR

Michael Dahl is the author of more than 200 books for children and young adults. He has won the AEP Distinguished Achievement Award three times for his nonfiction. His Finnegan Zwake mystery series was shortlisted twice by the Anthony and Agatha awards. He has also written the *Library of Doom* series. He is a featured speaker at conferences around the country on graphic novels and high-interest books for boys.

GLOSSARY

allies (AL-eyez)—people or countries that give support to each other

clung (KLUNG)—held onto something tightly

creature (KREE-chur)—a living thing that is human or animal

fierce (FEERSS)—violent, strong, or dangerous

gripping (GRIP-ing)—holding onto something very tightly

rule (ROOL)—have power over something

swerve (SWURV)—change direction quickly

swirling (SWURL-ing)—moving in circles

throb (THROB)—to beat loudly or rapidly

DISCUSSION QUESTIONS

1. If you were Will, would you have been afraid of the dragon?

2. Who was the dragon? What clues help you figure this out?

3. Have you ever been caught in a storm? What was it like? How did you feel?

WRITING PROMPTS

1. Imagine Will tries to figure out more about the dragon. Write a short story about his adventure.

2. Dragons are mythical creatures. Write a story about another mythical creature.

3. The title of a book can attract readers, as well as provide a description of the story. Think of three new titles for this book, choose your favorite, and explain why it's your pick.

INTERNET SITES

The book may be over, but the adventure is just beginning.

Do you want to read more about the subjects or ideas in this book? Want to play cool games or watch videos about the authors who write these books? Then go to FactHound. At *www.facthound.com,* you'll be able to do all that, and more. The FactHound website can also send you to other safe Internet sites.

Check it out!

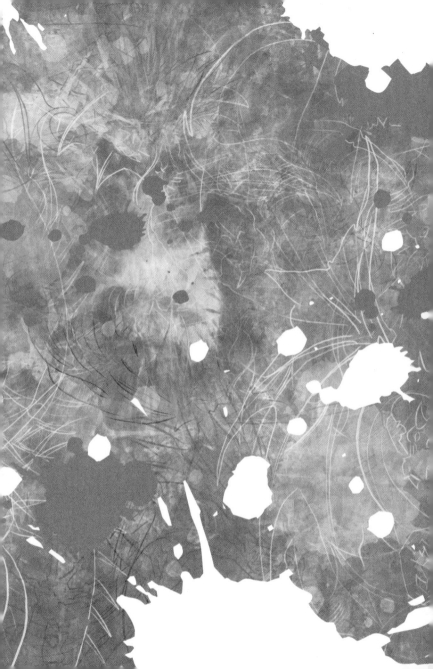

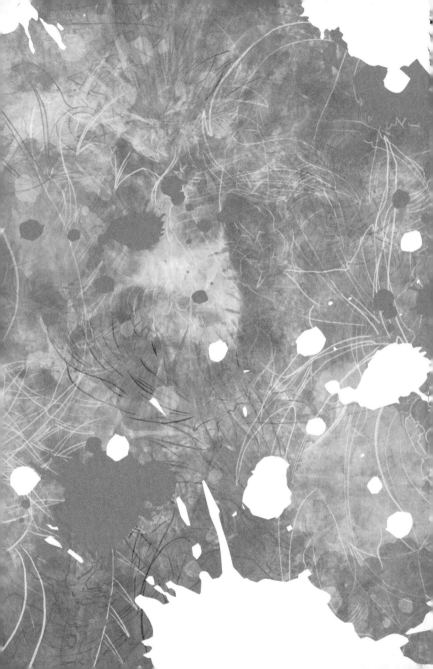